Time Warp Trio™ is produced by WGBH in association with Soup2Nuts for Discovery Kids.

Harper Trophy® is a registered trademark of HarperCollins Publishers.

Time Warp Trio®
Time Warp Trio: Lewis and Clark . . . and Jodie, Freddi, and Samantha
Library of Congress catalog card number: 2006924547
ISBN-10: 0-06-111638-6 — ISBN-13: 978-0-06-111638-4

Typography by Joe Merkel
❖
First Harper Trophy edition, 2006

Lewis and Clark...
and JODIE, FREDDI,
and SAMANTHA

Time Warp Trio created by
Jon Scieszka
Adapted by
Jennifer Frantz
Based on the television script by
Gentry Menzel

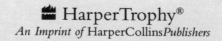

HarperTrophy®
An Imprint of HarperCollinsPublishers

CHAPTER 1

"**G**reat. Just great," I said, pulling a twig from my hair. "I told you to stop messing with *The Book*."

"You definitely didn't, Jodie," Samantha said. "You told me to stop getting marshmallow all over it."

Leave it to Samantha to get specific at a time like this. Thanks to *her* sticky, marshmallowy fingers we were now stuck in a shrub in Rocky Mountain–nowhere, three hundred years back in time.

"Excuse me," I said. "You're right. Next time I say that, what I really mean is— STOP MESSING WITH *THE BOOK*." After landing in a bush, my hair was totally dreadful, and so was my mood.

"Fine," Samantha said. "I'll never touch *The Book* again, and *you* can't touch my cat."

"That's a promise," I said. Did she really think I cared about her silly metal cyberpet? We're talking about a tin cat that ate thumbtacks.

Samantha was about to say something back, when Freddi interrupted. "Uh, guys," she said. "Could you look at this?"

Freddi seemed worried—as usual. She motioned Samantha and me toward a clearing in the brush.

"Hey, it's *The Book*!" Samantha cried.

"And my backpack," I said, spying the pink mound a few feet away.

"Yeah," Freddi said. "And also . . . *a bear*!"

"AAAAAAAAAGHHHHHHHHHH!" Samantha and I screamed.

There it was—a giant grizzly bear—smack-dab in the middle of the clearing. It was rooting around near my backpack and . . . *The Book*!

Samantha, Freddi, and I dove back to our bush and hid in the spindly branches.

"Don't move. Don't even breathe," I whispered.

We had to find a way to grab *The Book* and get back home—and becoming a bear buffet was definitely *not* part of the plan.

The grizzly was sniffing around my backpack. He must have smelled something tasty inside. I just hoped he wasn't going to get his nasty bear-slobber all over everything.

Meanwhile, Freddi pointed out a bigger problem. The bear was lowering his big furry bottom toward the sticky marshmallow-covered book.

"Don't sit on *The Book*. Don't sit on *The Book*," Freddi whispered.

Just our luck . . . the bear sat on *The Book*. And thanks to the marshmallow goo all over the cover, it immediately stuck to his fur.

"Okay," I whispered. "Who wants to ask that nice bear to move his butt? Samantha?"

Samantha did get us into this mess after all. But apparently she was too busy getting a case of the hiccups.

"Hic," she blurted loudly. The bear turned his huge, mean face in our direction. I guess even grizzly bears know that bushes don't get the hiccups.

"Shhhhhhh," Freddi and I whispered.

"I can't just . . . *hic* . . ." Samantha tried to talk between the hiccups. "I need to . . . *hic* . . . drink some water . . . *hic* . . . or stand on my head . . .

hic . . . or get really, really scared."

Suddenly, the bear poked his head—sharp teeth and all—through the bush and let out a huge *ROOOOOOOOAAAAAR* that shook the branches.

"AAAAAAAGHHH!" we all screamed at once.

We scrambled out of the bush and ducked behind a nearby boulder. Freddi and I tried to catch our breath.

"Hey! It worked," Samantha said. "My hiccups are gone."

"Well, that's just super," I said. Peering around the edge of the boulder, I saw the bear rooting around my backpack again. *The Book* was still stuck to his bottom.

"Okay," I said. "Let's not panic. Bears are pretty dumb, right? It's not like we're facing a crazed mountain man or anything."

Suddenly, Samantha, Freddi, and I heard a twig snap behind us.

"Don't move," a voice commanded.

We turned and saw a man in old-fashioned mountaineer clothing. He held a huge rifle . . . that was pointed at us!

"*Hic,*" Samantha blurted.

But something told me Samantha's hiccups were the least of our worries.

CHAPTER 2

Okay. So you may be wondering how we got into such a colossal mess. It's simple— marshmallows.

See, Samantha, Freddi, and I were all camping. But in the year 2105, you'd call it cybercamping, since we weren't really outside or anything messy like that. We'd dialed up a beachy scene with a bonfire and had begun roasting marshmallows.

"Umm, mmm," Samantha said. "There's nothing better than a toasted marshmallow."

I'm not sure if she had actually tasted it, or

if she was just wearing it. She was covered from head to toe in white sticky mush.

I looked down at my own marshmallow. "I think there's sand in mine," I said. "And the salt air is totally squenching my hair."

Our beach backdrop was starting to feel a bit too "natural" for my taste. "Let's see," I said, reaching for the control panel. "Camping Options . . . Seaside . . . Woods . . . Backyard . . . Desert." I selected Woods, which sounded much less gritty and damp than our current beach setting.

In a flash, the beach landscape melted away. We were now surrounded by green grass, tall trees, and the sound of owls hooting.

"Ah . . . much better," I said. "This Camp-Master 3000 Omni-Projection System is so chair. I just love how . . ."

But suddenly, my lovely mellow thought

was interrupted by the sound of a cat—*peeing*.

I glared at Samantha. "That better not be your cat."

"Bad kitty," Samantha pretend-scolded. "I told you not to pee on Jodie's grass."

Leave it to Samantha's cat to totally ruin a nice moment.

At least Freddi didn't seem to mind. She was staring up at the sky with a dreamy look. "You know," she said, "in the olden days, people used to sleep in bags in the woods."

"Sleep outside?" I asked. "On purpose?" Was that supposed to be fun, or some sort of punishment?

"I bet it was really magical, camping out under the stars," Freddi said.

Samantha and I both burst into laughter at the thought of fraidy-cat-Freddi sleeping outside.

"Freddi, you would *hate* that," Samantha said. "You'd be scared to death."

"Is that an ant?" I teased in my best Freddi voice. *"Get it off! Get it OFF!"*

"I'm not that bad," Freddi said. "And it's spiders I don't like. . . . And moths . . . and worms . . . and . . ."

"Hey," Samantha said. "I have an idea. Let's try it. Let's go camping for real."

Before Freddi or I could say anything, Samantha grabbed *The Book* from my backpack. Now this was not just any book. I had inherited it from my great grandfather, Joe, who lived in the twenty-first century. It could take you to any place and time. While that sounds really cool, there was one problem: Whenever we traveled back in time, *The Book* had a habit of disappearing. And without it, there was no way to get back home.

Samantha opened up *The Book* to the Where/When Web page and began poking the keys with her sticky fingers.

"Be careful," I said. "You're getting marshmallow all over *The Book*."

"Sorry," Samantha said, licking her hand. "Okay. Let's search for 'camping' and 'girls' and 'woods,' and see what we get."

Samantha hit the enter key, and results were up on the screen in a flash.

"Here we go," she cried. "*Corps of Discovery, 1805, Rocky Mountains.* I wonder what that is?"

"Camping in 1805?" I said. "I don't think so." Let's be honest, I could barely handle camping in 2105—in my own bedroom.

Samantha tried to move the cursor down the page to check out our other options, but her gooey fingers got stuck. A big string of

marshmallow stretched from Samantha's hand to *The Book*.

"Where did this come from?" Samantha said. She began to pull harder and harder. The marshmallow string snapped like a rubber band . . . and hit *The Book* with a loud *bing*!

"Oh, no," Freddi said. "You hit enter!"

The familiar green mist began to spew from *The Book*. I yanked it from Samantha and tried pounding the cancel key as quickly as I could.

"Cancel, cancel, cancel!" I yelled.

But it was too late. The green mist was taking us camping—for real.

CHAPTER 3

So that's how we got to the Rocky Mountains in 1805, where we'd already been chased by a bear, and were now staring down the rifle of a crazed mountain man. See? I told you. Marshmallows can be *very* dangerous.

Freddi, Samantha, and I stood frozen in place behind the boulder.

"I've got you now," the mountain man bellowed. I held my breath. This was it. He raised his rifle and took aim—at the bear!

The shot missed the grizzly by inches.

But it scared him enough to drop my backpack and run off.

"Dang. Missed him," the man said.

"Oh, no," Freddi said. "The bear's taking *The Book*."

She was right. *The Book* was still stuck to the bear's behind, and now he was getting away.

"Hey, bear," I yelled. "Give that back!"

I took off after the bear, determined to get *The Book*. Soon I was just a few feet away from him. If only I could reach just a little bit farther I could grab—

"AAAHHHHHH!" I screamed. The bear had spun around. He showed his huge teeth and swiped at me with razor-sharp claws.

I jumped behind Samantha. The grizzly let out a final growl and lumbered off into the woods.

The mountain man looked at us, confused. "You girls must really like to read," he said.

"No," Freddi tried to explain. "It's just a very special book."

"Well, don't worry," the man said. "He'll be back. That bear's been doggin' us for days, trying to get our food."

Then he hoisted his rifle to his shoulder and began to walk off. Freddi, Samantha, and I just stood there.

"Now what?" Freddi asked.

"Well, we have to get *The Book* back," Samantha said. "Otherwise we're stuck here for, um . . . let's see . . . forever."

Freddi looked worried.

I could see it was time for action. "Well,

I say we follow that man and hope the bear gets hungry real soon."

I grabbed my backpack—which was luckily free of bear slobber—and Samantha, Freddi, and I hiked off into the woods toward certain doom.

CHAPTER 4

The not-crazed-mountain-man, named York, led us into a busy camp. Men were rushing this way and that, taking down tents and packing supplies onto horses.

A rugged-looking man wearing a fringed animal-skin coat was sitting on a rock. He was sketching a grizzly bear, just like the one we'd seen. The man kept drawing as we walked toward him.

"Get that bear, York?" he asked, without looking up.

"No, I'm sorry, Mr. Lewis," York said. "I missed him again."

"Dang," the man said.

Finally, the man gazed up from his drawing. He seemed surprised to see three girls in his camp. "Who are you?" he asked.

"I'm Jodie," I said. "This is Samantha and Freddi. We were out walking, and we . . . got lost." I hoped it sounded believable.

The man scratched his head. "Well, it's an odd place to be walking, but welcome to the Corps of Discovery. I'm Meriwether Lewis and that gentleman over there is Mr. William Clark," he said, pointing to a man with a large mustache.

"No way," Samantha gasped. "*The* Lewis and Clark? The famous explorers?"

"Famous?" Mr. Lewis snorted. "We'll be *dead* explorers if we don't get over this mountain by tomorrow."

"Why? What's the hurry?" Samantha asked.

"The *hurry* is that it's late September," Mr. Lewis said. "Once the snows start, we'll freeze to death. Or starve. Or both."

York heaved Mr. Lewis's pack onto his shoulder. "It's a good thing you gals showed up when you did," York said. "We're gonna need all the help we can get."

Freeze . . . starve . . . help? Were these people serious? I looked at Samantha and Freddi. Suddenly sandy marshmallows were looking like . . . well . . . a day at the beach.

CHAPTER 5

Before we could even stop to rest, the entire camp was on the move—including Samantha, Freddi, and me. We quickly found ourselves trudging up a steep mountain path. Gigantic heavy packs, which were neither cute nor pink, were strapped to our backs.

With each painful step, I was getting more annoyed with Samantha and her stupid sticky fingers. Finally I exploded. "But noooooo . . . You couldn't bring us to the successful, we're-almost-there Lewis and Clark. You bring us to the *near-death* Lewis and Clark."

"Look," Samantha said. "As soon as we get *The Book*, we can go home. Plus . . . we *are* camping!"

This was no time to start looking on the bright side. "We're pack animals," I said. "Pack animals who are ruining our—*oof*—" At that moment, I tripped over a pesky rock. "Shoes."

I looked down. It was true—my favorite pair of very cute, very pink shoes were covered in scuffs and mud.

Suddenly, a Native American girl appeared. She must have been about seventeen years old. She glanced down at my shoes. "Those are beautiful *biga-nambe*," she said. "But they cannot be good for mountain walking."

I looked over at her shoes. She was wearing a pair of thick brown moccasins. I guess that's what she considered a sensible pair of *biga-nambe*.

The girl was lugging a pack even bigger than ours. She was clearly one tough chick.

"Who are you?" I asked.

"I am Sacagawea," she said.

Freddi's face lit up. "I know who you are," she said. "You're Lewis and Clark's translator."

"Actually," Sacagawea said, "my husband is the translator. I assist him. But how could you have heard of me?"

"I did a report on you in American history cla—" Freddi started to say, when I elbowed her in the ribs.

"What she meant to say," I interrupted, "is 'Hi, my name is Freddi, and this is Jodie, and that's Samantha.'"

"It is a pleasure to meet you," Sacagawea replied.

Suddenly, we heard a baby fussing. Sacagawea turned around. Slung across her back in a cloth sling was a tiny baby.

"Oh," Sacagawea said. "This is Jean-Baptiste, my son. But we call him Little Pomp."

"You're camping . . . with a *baby*?" I said. "A baby who cries and poops and stuff?"

"Yes," Sacagawea replied. "But Pomp rarely cries. Mostly he's happy."

Sacagawea started walking to catch up with the group. Freddi, Samantha, and I followed.

"I'm glad you have joined us," Sacagawea said. "It will be nice to talk to girls for a change."

Even though she was a hard-core mountaineering mama, Sacagawea was still a girl after all. Except for our taste in shoes, we weren't *so* different. . . .

"I know what you mean," I told her. "Guys never get what's important. Like when you have a total hair emergency." I pulled some more bush debris out of my tragic hair.

"Oh," Sacagawea responded. "I was hoping we might talk about hunting, or cooking, or caring for a baby. . . ."

Okay, so maybe we *were* so different. . . .

"Sometimes," she added, "I feel a little lonely, even though there are many people here."

"I feel the same way," Freddi said. "How did you end up on this trip anyway?"

"I am Shoshone," Sacagawea said. "When I was twelve, I was kidnapped by another tribe and taken far away. They sold me to the man who is now my husband. Later we met Mr. Lewis and Mr. Clark, and they chose my husband and me to be their translators."

"You were stolen from your family?" Freddi gasped. "That's horrible."

Sacagawea looked sad for a moment, then smiled. "Jean-Baptiste is my family now. I could ask for no more."

We all gazed as Sacagawea adjusted the tiny bundle in the drooping cloth sling. "Except," she said, "for a better way to carry him."

A small stream crossed our path, and Sacagawea hopped across nimbly—pack, baby, and all. Then it was my turn. I did my best jump, but landed right in the water. Typical.

"Well," Samantha said, smiling, "at least your shoes are clean."

Leave it to Samantha to find something funny about my completely soaked, absolutely ruined, formerly adorable shoes.

We hiked on, following Sacagawea and the group farther up the mountain. As the sun sank lower in the sky, I couldn't help thinking of Mr. Lewis's warning. If we didn't make it to the top by sundown, we'd all be . . . dead.

CHAPTER 6

After several hours, we stumbled into camp. Literally. My feet were throbbing and swollen.

"I am through with walking," I announced. "When I get back home I am disking *everywhere*."

Samantha and I sat down to rub our aching feet, while Freddi fed sticks into the campfire.

"Want to hear the good news?" Freddi asked. "Sacagawea is bringing us some food."

Samantha's eyes lit up at the mention of food. "Great," she said. "We'll eat until we're full, then use the leftovers as bear bait."

Sacagawea arrived carrying three tin plates. "Here. I hope you will like this," she said, handing a plate to each of us.

We were ready for serious feasting. But looking down at our plates, we saw only one tiny blob of who-knows-what. Some sort of corn mush with grayish meaty bits on top.

"It is the last of our food," Sacagawea explained. "But when we cross the mountain, we will find the Nez Perce and then we can trade with them for more."

I had no idea what she was talking about. But that's why I'm friends with Samantha.

"The Nez Perce is another tribe of Native Americans. They traveled across Washington, Oregon, and Idaho," Samantha whispered to me.

"I also made a place for you to sleep," Sacagawea said.

Ahh, sleep. At least *that* would be good.

Sacagawea pointed to a shabby canvas tent covering a few blankets on the cold, hard ground. My heart sank. I looked at Samantha. Apparently even she had stopped looking on the bright side.

"Um . . . thank you," Freddi said. "Thanks for everything."

Good old Freddi.

"You are welcome," Sacagawea said. "Oh, there's one more thing."

Sacagawea pulled a small tin from her pocket. In a flash, she was spreading nasty goo all over my head.

"What are you doing?" I cried.

"This is bear grease," she said. "It will take all of the emergencies out of your hair."

Emergencies? Now my hair was in a grease-covered state of total trauma!

Sacagawea added one final glob of goo, then turned to go. "Now I must feed the men and attend to Little Pomp," she said. "Good night."

Freddi and Samantha stared over at my slimy new do.

"Not a *word*. Not one word," I said.

I was tired, greasy, and starving. I actually thought about eating the mouthful of mystery mush on my plate. But one sniff quickly changed my mind. Time for Plan B. I moved the tin plate aside and grabbed my backpack.

"I wonder what that bear left?" I said. Rooting through the pockets, I found something. "Oooh! A Mondo Chocko bar."

Success.

But before I had one sweet Chocko–licious bite, Samantha snatched the candy away.

"The bear will love this," she said. "As soon as he comes close enough, we'll grab *The Book*, go home, and you can get another Mondo bar. Okay?"

Okay? I was supposed to give my last piece of food to a bear that had tried to kill me. Not okay, but, as much as I hated to admit it, Samantha did have a point. If we were ever going to get out of here, we had to get *The Book* back.

The sky turned from purple to black, and the moon peeked out from behind some pine trees. One by one, stars began to twinkle in the sky.

"Hey, Freddi," I said. "Here come your stars."

Within minutes, the whole sky was filled

with them. Real twinkling stars. I had to admit, it *was* kind of pretty. Freddi, Samantha, and I sat quietly.

The silence was broken, suddenly, by a blood-curdling coyote howl. Samantha, Freddi, and I dove into the tent faster than you can say "Big Dipper."

Never mind going to bed without dinner. Now we just wanted to go to bed without *becoming* dinner.

But in the middle of the night, Freddi and I were still wide awake. Between our less-than-cozy tent and Samantha snoring like a lumberjack, sleeping was impossible.

"If only she came with an off switch," I whispered to Freddi.

A moment later, we heard a noise outside our tent. Something was out there.

"Did you hear that?" I asked.

Then we heard a wrapper crinkling.

"It's the bear," Freddi said. "He's found the Mondo bar."

Sleeping Beauty Samantha heard the commotion and suddenly awoke. Energized by news of the bear, she threw off her blanket and leapt out of the tent.

"Is that you, bear?" she said. "You can have the candy, just give me *The* . . ."

GRRRRRRRRRRRRRRR.

The bear let out a deafening roar. He must not have appreciated Samantha interrupting his midnight snack. Samantha came flying back into the tent and dove under a blanket. Finally, she poked her head out.

"He didn't want to give it back," she said.

A disgusting smell hit my nose. "What's going on?" I said to Samantha. "You *stink*."

"Oh, yeah," Samantha said, sniffing her arm. "There was a skunk out there, too."

"Aaaaaaahhhhhhh!" I screamed, diving under a different blanket.

Huddled in the smelly tent in the freezing cold, I could only imagine what the next day would bring. Only one thing was certain— I was afraid to find out.

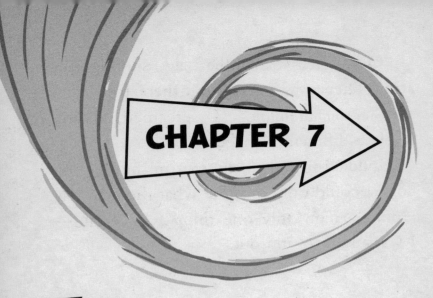

CHAPTER 7

The next morning, I awoke to the sounds of Samantha snoring and Freddi chattering on about something.

"Wake up!" she cried. "It's the most beautiful thing you ever saw."

After my night of terrible sleep, the only thing I wanted to see was my therma-spa, full of hot water and lots of bubbles.

Freddi threw open the tent so I could get a peek outside.

"You have *got* to be kidding," I said. "Snow?"

Sure enough, there was a fresh coating of the cold white stuff covering every inch of ground.

"Look at the treetops," Freddi gushed. "They look like lace."

"I am *not* trudging through snow," I said. "No way, no how." Trekking up a mountain weighed down like a mule was bad enough. Trekking up a mountain weighed down like a mule *in snow* was simply out of the question.

I felt a nervous breakdown coming on.

Mr. Clark approached the tent and looked to Freddi and a very groggy Samantha.

"Is your friend okay?" he asked, sensing my distress.

"Yeah, she's fine," Samantha said. "She's just not too thrilled about the snow."

"I thought the grizzlies were givin' us a hard time," Clark replied. "But this snow beats all. We have got to get to the other side of this mountain. Today."

The mountain he was talking about was: (a) enormous, (b) far away, and (c) covered in— you guessed it—SNOW.

"Isn't there some shortcut we could take?" Samantha suggested. "I mean—did you check a map?"

"Map?" Clark said with a laugh. "There is no map. I'm drawing it as we go."

He pulled out a large piece of rolled-up paper and opened it. The right and left sides of the map were filled in with the names of states, major landforms, and bodies of water. But the middle part of the map was practically empty, except for some recent sketches. Clark was filling in the map as the group traveled.

"See," Clark said, pointing to a river on the filled-in part of the map. "If we can just get to the Columbia River, we'll be Yankee doodle dandy. It's a trading route, so we can grab ourselves a couple of canoes and paddle to the Pacific. And then, that's it—we're done."

"Except for the gettin'-back-home part," he added as he rolled up the map.

The scary news was starting to sink in: We were in totally uncharted territory.

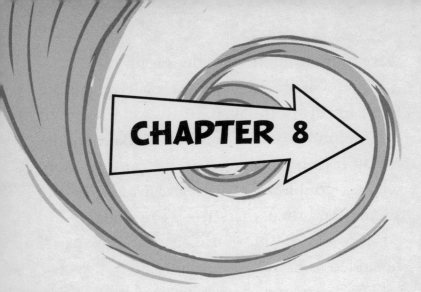

CHAPTER 8

"**H**ey guys, look what I got," I said proudly, showing Samantha and Freddi my newest find—a horse. If we were going to trek through this silly snow, we might as well ride in style.

Samantha and Freddi were thrilled to see the horse and scrambled up onto his back. We fell in line with the rest of the Corps of Discovery, who had begun to climb a steep cliff.

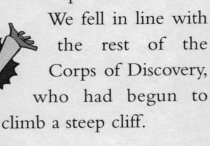

Samantha was enjoying the ride. "How'd you get this horse anyway?" she asked.

"Well," I said, "I just explained to Mr. Lewis that I couldn't walk another step, and *voila*—instant horse."

"Jodie," Samantha said. "Sometimes I'm glad you're you."

As we climbed higher, the mountain got steeper and the path grew narrower. Freddi peered over the sharp ledge and a queasy look came over her.

"Why do mountains have to be so high?" she whimpered.

Then suddenly we heard a deep growl.

"Did you hear that?" I asked. The horse must have heard it, too. He started to neigh nervously.

"It's the bear! It's gotta be," Samantha said. "Go back. I think I can see him."

I tried to wheel the horse around, but he was scared and didn't want to go.

"Does the bear still have *The Book*?" I asked Samantha, staring up at the mountain where she was looking.

"Uh, guys . . . *guys*!" Freddi cried.

The horse's back foot had slipped over the edge of the cliff. Suddenly the horse started to slide farther down.

"We're goin' down!" Samantha screamed.

The horse's front feet were still on the path, but his back feet were scrambling over the ledge. To make matters worse, the path was beginning to crumble.

The horse jolted, and Freddi fell off the front. She landed with a thud on the ground. But Samantha and I were stuck, clinging desperately to the scared, unsteady horse. More path crumbled and the horse's hooves fell farther down the ledge.

It looked like Freddi was going to be warping solo from now on.

CHAPTER 9

In a flash, Sacagawea was racing to our rescue. She placed Little Pomp down in a safe spot and grabbed our horse's reins.

"*Deche . . . deche . . . ,*" she whispered softly to the frightened horse.

I hoped her horse whispering was better than her hairstyling.

But no luck! The horse was too scared to calm down. His feet scrambled farther down the ledge—sending Samantha and I lurching a few feet closer to doom.

"The saddle," Sacagawea said to Freddi.

"Grab the saddle."

They pulled with all their might. Freddi struggled as she threw her puny body into it. Tugging steadily, Sacagawea continued to soothe the horse. "*Deche . . . dee-daga . . . quiet . . . friend . . .*"

Slowly the horse calmed down and began to regain his footing. Guided by Freddi and Sacagawea, he made his way carefully back onto solid ground.

Samantha and I let out the deep breaths we'd been holding. The entire Corps, who had gathered around us, let out a cheer.

"Thank you, Sacagawea," Mr. Lewis said.

"This is not the first time you have proven your worth."

"But you must thank Freddi, too," Sacagawea said modestly. Then she turned to Samantha and me. "I am sorry, for my horse is not usually so clumsy."

"*Your* horse?" Freddi cried. "We took *your* horse?"

"Yes, well, you seemed to need the help," Sacagawea replied.

Freddi glared at me. I felt my cheeks go warm and red.

"Thanks," I said to Sacagawea. "But we're all rested now, so you should definitely have your horse back. You've been carrying all your stuff, and a baby, and . . ." I gulped. I saw my pink backpack strapped to the huge mound Sacagawea had been carrying on her back. "And all of *our* stuff, too."

"Here, give us some of that," Freddi said.

Samantha, Freddi, and I divided up Sacagawea's huge load. I heaved my share onto my back.

"Okay, that's a bit heavier than it looks," I said.

Sacagawea made a move to help me.

"But it's *totally* fine," I said. "I'm never going to complain again. If you can do it, so can I."

Sacagawea picked up Little Pomp and mounted her horse. "Thank you," she said. "I will scout ahead for food."

She rode off, and Samantha, Freddi, and I began to trudge up the snowy path.

The slippery ground and the heavy packs quickly grew tiresome.

"We have got to get *The Book*," I said, "because there is no way I can do this without complaining."

But Samantha and Freddi didn't seem to be listening. They were too busy thinking about the stupid bear.

"I wonder if we could call to him?" Samantha said.

"You know bear calls?" Freddi asked.

"No," Samantha admitted. "But I'm great at yelling. Let's see, if I were a bear, I'd make a sound like . . ."

Samantha cleared her throat. I knew we were in for something.

"SNEEEERRROOOOOOOOOO! BWAAAAAEEEEEEEEE! SNAR-HUNKA-HUNKA-RRRRRR!" Samantha bellowed.

A noise like that probably scared every creature for one hundred miles.

"You are insane. You know that?" I said.

"Well," a voice said, "she wouldn't be the first explorer to go off her rocker." It was York.

"No really, I'm fine," Samantha explained. "I was just doing bear calls."

"Bears don't answer calls," York said. "The only thing that'll bring a bear is food."

"Which we don't have," Freddi pointed out.

"No," said York. "But we will . . . just as soon as we make it over this mountain."

The mountain. I wish people would stop reminding me.

Picking up the pace, York walked on ahead of us.

"Lewis and Clark *did* make it over the mountain . . . right?" Freddi asked nervously.

"Right," Samantha said. "But that was before *we* joined them."

CHAPTER 10

I'm not complaining, I'm not complaining, I thought with each painful step. But if I *were* complaining, I might say that this was the most annoying day of my entire life. We'd been hiking straight up a mountain for hours in the blinding, freezing snow, and we still hadn't reached . . .

"The top!" Clark yelled. "We've reached the top!"

The top? Could it really be?

Samantha, Freddi, and I raced the rest of the way until we reached the ledge where Clark was standing.

"Welcome to the new America, girls," he said, gesturing to the view.

"It's so beautiful," Freddi said.

"It's so magnificent," Samantha added.

"Isn't there a road somewhere?" I asked. "Or a truck stop? A rest area? A picnic table?"

Freddi and Samantha gave me a look.

Clark made a final scribble on his map. "Now all we have to do is find that river," Clark said. "Ok, men . . . and ladies. Move on."

Finally we staggered into camp. Dumping our packs, we warmed up by the campfire.

"Oh, thank you, Corps, for stopping," Samantha said.

"I'm going to lie right here, on my back, for the rest of my life," I said.

"Who are those guys?" Freddi asked.

I raised my head to see what she was looking at. Lewis and Clark were talking with two Native American men who were pointing to a canoe filled with bags.

Sacagawea joined us by the fire.

"What's going on?" Freddi asked her.

"That's Chief Twisted Hair of the Nez Perce," Sacagawea explained. "We're trading for canoes . . . and food."

"Food?" Samantha said. "Hot dog!"

"No," Sacagawea said. "We will not be serving dog, but fish and roots. And berries, if we can find some. Would you girls like to go look around with me?"

"I would," I said. "I really would, but I can't." I was taking my promise to lie there forever very seriously.

Samantha didn't seem too eager to move, either. "Now that there's food," she said, "maybe we should stay here. That bear might show up."

"I'll come," Freddi said.

Good old Freddi.

Samantha and I rested around the fire until we regained our strength. Soon the smell of food began to fill the camp. Lewis and Clark's trading must have been a success. My stomach started to growl.

"Speaking of growling," Samantha said, "where is that bear? Shouldn't he be here by now? There's food all over the place."

I decided to eat something before Samantha made me give my next meal to the bear. There were some berries on a bush nearby. I couldn't believe Sacagawea had missed them. I popped a few into my mouth.

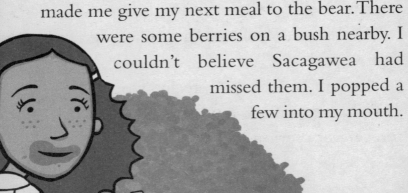

"Are you sure you should be eating those?" Samantha asked.

"Why not? They're delicious," I said, and gobbled down another handful.

Just then Sacagawea and Freddi returned.

"What are you doing?" Sacagawea cried. "Those berries will make you sick."

Sick? I spit chewed-up berries in every direction. But I already feared the worst. Was that a fever I felt coming on? Hives? A coma?

"I'm sick," I cried. "I'm extremely ill!"

Freddi took my hand. "Come on," she said. "Let's go see Mr. Lewis. He must have some medicine."

It took all my strength to follow Freddi over to where Mr. Lewis and Mr. Clark were seated. Mr. Clark was busy working on his map, while Mr. Lewis was sketching a new type of plant he'd found.

"Excuse me," Freddi said. "Mr. Lewis? Do you have anything for a stomachache? Jodie doesn't feel well."

"As it happens, I do," Mr. Lewis said. He reached over and picked up his medicine case. Inside the big wooden box were lots of small glass vials filled with who knows what. It was like something out of an old smelly museum.

"We have all the latest treatments," Mr. Lewis said. "Hmm . . . Let's see . . ."

Mr. Lewis rooted around in the box and pulled out a small brown vial. "I could give you an emetic," he said.

"Sure, sounds great," I replied. I had no idea what he was talking about.

"What's an emetic?" I whispered to Freddi.

"It makes you throw up," she whispered back.

Throw up? No thanks. "What else do you have?" I asked Mr. Lewis.

"I could drain some of your blood," Mr. Lewis said, holding up a small but very sharp-looking knife.

"Tempting," I said. "But no."

Next Mr. Lewis pulled out a bottle labeled RUSH'S THUNDERBOLTS. This looked promising. At least it was a name brand.

"What's that one?" I asked.

"Rush's Thunderbolts," Mr. Lewis said. "This'll go through your system like lightning. It'll make you, uh . . . "

Mr. Lewis turned a little red. Then he leaned down to whisper the totally drastic side effects. Let's just say in a place without real bathrooms *or* toilet paper, a slow death by poison berries was looking better and better.

"You know," I said, "I'm feeling much better. I think I'll just . . ."

Suddenly we heard Samantha scream. "Jodie! Freddi! Hurry!"

Freddi and I looked at each other. It could only mean one thing. "The bear!" we screamed.

We took off as fast as we could.

Back at our campsite, Samantha was sitting still as a stone, just a few feet away from the giant bear. Luckily, the bear's attention was on the big black pot he was eating from. Mr. Lewis and Mr. Clark ran up behind Freddi and me, and Sacagawea and York arrived seconds later. Everyone had heard Samantha's screams.

"Not to bother you," Samantha squeaked. "But . . . *help*."

"Rifles," Mr. Clark whispered. "We need rifles."

Mr. Lewis and York ran off. Sensing the commotion, the bear threw aside the pot and reared up on his hind legs. He was even bigger and meaner when standing up. He turned toward Samantha. She let out a terrified scream.

Freddi and I had to act fast. We had only a few seconds before our friend became grizzly grub.

CHAPTER 11

Freddi jumped into action. She grabbed the pot lid that was lying on the ground and a big rock.

"Aaaaaaahhhhhhh!" she screamed and ran toward the bear, clanging the pot lid loudly with the rock.

"Freddi, no!" I yelled. Something told me this was not the best way to calm down an angry bear.

Even the bear looked confused for a minute. Then he made an angry swipe at Freddi's head. She ducked just in time and kept right on with her banging and yelling.

Mr. Lewis returned with a rifle and got off a shot. It whizzed past Freddi and missed the bear.

"Dang," Mr. Lewis said, quickly reloading his gun.

Freddi, meanwhile, was banging and yelling louder than ever. The crazy thing was—it was starting to work.

The bear dropped to all fours and slowly began to lumber away. As he turned, we could see *The Book* was still stuck to his butt.

"There it is!" I cried. "*The Book!*"

Mr. Lewis took another shot at the bear and missed again.

"Dang," he said. "Oh, well. At least we scared him off."

For a moment we were all relieved. But then I screamed, "The bear is running away . . . with *The Book!*"

"Come on!" Freddi cried and took off after the bear.

Samantha and I were right behind her, and Sacagawea was right behind us.

"What are you doing?" she yelled. "Never run after a bear. He will kill you!"

"We have to get that book," Freddi yelled back. "It's our only way home."

The bear stopped at the edge of a creek. We had him trapped—or so we thought. The bear took one look at crazed, charging Freddi, and he shimmied up a tree.

"Now we'll never get *The Book*," I wailed.

"Oh, yes we will," Freddi said. Without skipping a beat, she whipped the pot lid into the air. It whizzed toward the bear's bottom like a torpedo.

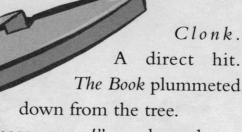

Clonk.

A direct hit. *The Book* plummeted down from the tree.

"Yaaaaaayyyyyy!" we cheered.

Until *The Book* fell . . . right in the creek.

"Noooooooooooo!" we yelled.

Suddenly Mr. Clark and York rushed up with a canoe. They tossed it into the river. Mr. Clark jumped into the front and Sacagawea jumped in the back.

"Come on!" she said.

Samantha, Freddi, and I hopped in, and we all paddled furiously after *The Book*.

Rough waters flung our canoe this way and that as we tried to keep sight of the bobbing book as it floated farther and farther away.

"Hold on," Mr. Clark yelled, skillfully guiding our canoe through the choppy current. Water splashed in our eyes. When I opened mine, all I could see was more fast rapids ahead.

"Woo-hoo!" I had to admit—it was kind of fun.

The canoe continued to bounce along, flying through the air and nearly tipping over. Just when I'd had enough, we turned a bend onto a big calm stretch of water.

I glanced over the wide, flat river—no ripples, no rapids, no book.

"Where's *The Book*?" I asked.

Suddenly Freddi spotted it fifty feet downstream. "There it is!" she cried.

Mr. Clark and Sacagawea powered the canoe closer and closer until we were alongside *The Book*. Freddi leaned over and plucked it out of the river.

"All right!" Samantha and I yelled.

"Do you know what this is?" Mr. Clark said excitedly.

Clearly he'd never seen a book quite like ours.

"Well, yeah," I said. "It's a book, only it's not a regular—"

"No," Mr. Clark interrupted. "The river. It's headin' west. I'll bet you anything it leads to the Columbia. *Wa-hooooo!*"

Mr. Clark was so excited that he jumped to his feet and promptly fell out of the canoe. It looked like he'd be able to finish his map after all.

Sacagawea swiftly spun the canoe around and paddled it over to the shore. Samantha, Freddi, and I hopped out onto the bank. Then Sacagawea stepped out and pulled the canoe out of the water.

A sopping wet, very happy Mr. Clark waded over to us. "Thank you, ladies," he said.

"If it weren't for you, I'm not sure we would've found this place."

Flipping his water-logged hat onto his head, he waved good-bye. "And now I'm off to tell the men."

Sacagawea looked over at Freddi, Samantha, and me. "I am glad that you have found your book," she said.

"Thanks, Sacagawea," Samantha said. "We couldn't have done it without you."

"We couldn't have done *anything* without you," Freddi added.

Sacagawea smiled. "But that is not true," she said. "You did many things. You saved my horse, you walked for miles in terrible shoes, you scared a bear, and you found your book."

Maybe we weren't so bad at roughing it after all. But I had to admit, I still missed the good ol' comforts of the twenty-second century. I opened *The Book* to prepare for our trip home.

Freddi's face lit up. "Jodie, give her your backpack."

"My backpack?" I said. "But there's nothing . . . Oh, right." I suddenly realized what Freddi wanted. "It's not much," I said, handing it to Sacagawea, "but we want you to have it . . . to thank you for all of your help."

Sacagawea looked confused.

"It'll be great for gathering berries," Freddi explained. "And maybe Little Pomp can ride in it."

A huge smile spread across Sacagawea's face. "*Aishenda'ga* . . . thank you," she said. "And thank you also for your friendship. I will miss you."

The Book was activated and the familiar green mist began to swirl around us.

Freddi waved to Sacagawea and said, "Good–bye. *Aishenda'ga* . . ."

Then we were gone.

CHAPTER 12

We rematerialized in the forest. Only this time, it was the year 2105 and the forest was comfortably located in my very own bedroom.

Everything was just as we'd left it—including Samantha's silly cat that was eating the leftover marshmallows.

"Oh, kitty," Samantha gushed. "Did you miss me?"

Of the many things I missed from home, Samantha's cat was not one of them.

"So," I said, "did Lewis and Clark ever find that river to the Pacific Ocean they were looking for?"

"No," Freddi said. "The Northwest Passage didn't really exist, but they did find lots of other things."

"Yeah," Samantha said, snuggling her cyberkitty, "like lots of new kinds of animals and plants."

"And maybe their best find of all was Sacagawea," Freddi added. "Without her, they might not have made it. She was able to get them horses and find them food. She even saved some important papers when someone tipped over a canoe."

"I wonder if it was Mr. Clark's map," I said.

"I don't know," said Freddi, "but without Lewis and Clark, there might still be a big empty space in our map today."

After hiking for hours, chasing down a bear, and nearly changing the course of American history, I was pooped.

"I don't know about you two," I said to Freddi and Samantha, "but I'm going to bed. G'night." If I never had to spend another sleepless night outdoors, it would be too soon.

I crawled into my
comfy, climate-controlled tent,
and Freddi and Samantha followed soon after.

"You know," Samantha said, "before we go
to sleep, there's something I want to say.
Freddi, you were totally amazing out there—
you really saved our butts."

It was true. Fraidy-cat-Freddi had been
really brave.

Freddi blushed. "Oh, well . . . it was kinda fun," she said. "But thanks."

"I have something to say, too," I announced.

"Yeah? What?" Samantha asked.

My stomach gurgled. "I *really* shouldn't have eaten those berries!"

It looked like we were in for another *very* long night.